Volume 1

Aesop's Fables

Stories by Ken Spillman

Art by Suvidha Mistry

SCHOLASTIC
New York Toronto London Auckland
Sydney New Delhi Hong Kong

Dr Ken Spillman is the author of more than 50 books including the internationally popular Jake series. Based in Australia, Ken travels frequently and has spoken to more than 70,000 children in the past four years. He is a long-time advocate for writers and writing in the Asian region and actively supports organisations connecting marginalised children with the world of stories. For more information, visit: www.kenspillman.com.

Suvidha Mistry is a freelance illustrator with a passion for all forms of art. She loves to tell stories with her illustrations, sketches and photographs. She has worked with multimedia firms as a graphic head and is now living her dream of being an illustrator of children's books.

Published by Scholastic India Pvt. Ltd.
A subsidiary of Scholastic Inc., New York, 10012 (USA).
Publishers since 1920, with international operations in Canada, Australia, New Zealand, the United Kingdom, India, and Hong Kong.

For information regarding permission, write to:
Scholastic India Pvt. Ltd.
A-27, Ground Floor, Sigma Centre
Infocity-1, Sector 34, Gurgaon 122001 (India)

First edition: April 2016
This reprint edition: December 2025

ISBN-13: 978-93-86041-02-9

Printed at Saurabh Printers Pvt. Ltd.

Introduction

Do you know that a person who writes fables is called a fabulist?

And that fables rank high among the most enduring stories of all time?

The fables of Aesop and the Panchatantra were both written more than 2,000 years ago, yet are still read by millions. The world may have changed, but we still find wisdom in these fine feats of fabulist imagination.

Why? Because a fable conveys a moral that can help us understand ourselves, as well as the people we encounter as we live our lives. Morals are better than even the most useful gadgets. Once absorbed, they are not only portable but invisible. Most don't go out of style and are guaranteed to last forever. How cool is that?

According to legend—and legends are legendary for being true, right?—Aesop was a far-from-handsome slave in ancient Greece. He gained his freedom by being clever!

Reading these stories inspired by Aesop's fabulous fables will not make you ugly, but it will certainly help make you clever.

Have some fun, readers!

Ken Spillman

Contents

The Frogs and their King

"We are all born equal," announced a big green frog to his peers. "That is the beauty of being amphibian."

He was holding forth on a lily pad and looked rather grand, his patterned skin glistening in the last of the day's sun. Although he wasn't quite the largest of the frogs in the pond, he had developed a habit of speaking with authority, puffing himself up with words.

"The beauty of being amphibian indeed!" his lady friend scoffed. "Only a frog would say that. Correction, only *you* would say something like that."

Around the pond, other frogs could be seen clinging to reeds, perched on sticks or squatting on lily pads like the pair

in conversation. A few were listening, though most were not. Among their number were many who rarely spoke a word, regarding words as indulgences in a world where it was far more important to keep watch for birds and snakes and tasty little flies. There were tadpoles to watch over, too—though it was well-nigh impossible to keep track of whose babies were whose.

"Big fellow," called a cheeky young frog who liked nothing better than challenging his elders. "You seem to think that equality is a blessing." This frog had decided while still a tadpole that he was brilliant—much too brilliant to be anybody's equal.

"Of course it is," replied the bigger of the two in his deep, gruff voice. "Don't you?"

"Well, perhaps you don't possess the vision to see how things might be better if they were different." Though the cheeky frog had never really considered this himself until now, he let his sentence hang in the air as if he had pondered it through many a long day.

"He's quite right," said the large frog's lady friend. "We should never simply assume that the way things *are* is exactly how they *should be*."

The large frog didn't seem to appreciate this contribution and shot her a disgruntled glance. He rearranged his toes on the lily pad before addressing his chief source of irritation directly.

"Tell me, then, if you must, how things might be better—in your own humble opinion, of course."

The younger frog had by now hit upon an idea which, like all his ideas, he felt sure was clever enough to announce to the world. He hadn't held the idea long enough in his head to actually *believe* in his clever words but, truth be told, *sounding* clever had always been more important to him than *being* clever.

"There is nothing wrong with equality," he began, "as long as there is leadership." Suddenly he noticed that almost all of the frogs around the pond had turned their heads to listen. This emboldened him further, and he projected his voice across the still water as if rallying imaginary troops.

"Our progress as a community depends on that and that alone, leadership. Unfortunately, we cling blindly to the belief that we frogs are all equal, which only means that we pay no heed to merit. In this pond, the best and brightest carry no sway over the dopy and dull-witted."

At this, many in his audience croaked and chirruped. Every frog, regardless of age or gender, felt certain that a list of the pond's best and brightest was bound to include them.

"What we need is a supreme being, a ruler who stands apart from us and quite above us. Under the sovereignty of a ruler, our pond would not be so, well..." He waved a front leg around, searching for the right word. "Our pond would not be so... *stagnant.*"

A couple of frogs gasped. Many nodded to each other. The large, proud frog gave out a low croak of displeasure.

"Hold your tongue, dear," urged his wife. "No need to turn this into an argument."

The younger frog was so very satisfied with his choice of word that he wanted immediately to repeat it. "Yes, friends, we are stagnant. Equality is pleasant, in its way, but who do we have to look up to? Without a ruler we have no direction."

The older frog could take this no more. "If you are so keen to be ruled, and to have the direction of a sovereign, why don't you see if the gods will oblige?"

"Very well," responded the cocky young frog. "As long as you remember that the gods do not *always* choose to make things easy for us. Whether they act in our interests is a matter for their wisdom."

"Of course," came the reply. "There is nothing more self-evident than that."

At that, the young frog called for a mighty chorus from all those who saw the good sense in asking the gods for a ruler. Together they raised their voices to the heavens, beseeching the gods to deliver them a monarch.

No sooner had they done so than a huge log splashed into the pond. It sent water flying and probably cost the lives of any number of poor tadpoles. Frogs darted away, terrified. For quite some time there was an awed silence.

"Long live the King," came the voice of the young frog who had led the chorus of prayer.

"Oh great and powerful King, we welcome you and thank the gods who sent you," said another.

Many other frogs called out to proclaim their loyalty, and even the large frog whose words had resulted in this astonishing event felt moved to speak.

His low, rumbling croak rang out across the pond. "As your subjects, good King, we are equals, and equally subject to your command."

The log, however, commanded nothing. The frogs suspected that the effort of falling and making such a gigantic splash might have exhausted him. They decided to let him rest.

Come the next day, however, the King was still at rest.

Come the next week, the unbroken rest of the monarch was beginning to cause *un*rest among the frogs.

"What kind of King is this?" one frog asked.

"Quite a wooden one," quipped another.

The large, green, outspoken frog had an idea. "Perhaps, my friends, our King has detected the perfection of our society and sees no reason for royal intervention. He wishes to be no more than a figurehead."

"Nonsense," laughed his lady friend. "Figurehead! Even a figurehead can listen, and this log is as deaf as a post. He's lazy, that's all. Can't even be bothered telling us his name."

"Maybe he's King Lazy the Third?" suggested a comedian in the group.

"What happened to the first two King Lazys?"

"In all probability, they are flat out ruling other ponds."

Even the young frog who had led the community in calling for a ruler laughed at this. He was bitterly disappointed with the gods and could not accept their choice of a king for his pond. They had embarrassed him and, though he knew it would seem ungrateful to beseech the gods again, saw no alternative. One morning, he attracted the attention of all the other frogs with a loud succession of high-pitched cawing sounds.

"With due respect to our beloved King, I think we would agree that his reign has not been all we hoped it might be." The young frog paused for a moment, appreciating the silent consent of his audience. "Monarchies thrive on timely succession. Perhaps now is the time for the gods to name a successor."

"This King is fine," croaked the large frog. "He lets us *be*—what more could we ask for?"

The young frog was not to be deterred. "He lets us be, that is true. He lets us be *mediocre*."

"Speak for yourself," the large frog croaked back.

The old fellow received a sharp kick from the powerful hind leg of his lady friend. "No need to be rude," she said.

Some frogs were nervous that the gods may be displeased if they were called upon to name another ruler for the pond

so soon. Yet the fact that the gods had obliged them once encouraged a belief that they might do so again, perhaps more satisfactorily.

The frogs raised their voices to the heavens once more. They cried out for leadership, for an active ruler who would truly stand above them, making waves and changing their pond world forever.

The gods were more than displeased about being pestered in this way, and cast down their wrath in the form of a heron.

Silence fell. The heron strutted along the log it had succeeded as ruler and the frogs bowed down before their new King.

"Sire, I am at your service," announced the cheeky young frog, keen to make a good first impression. "I welcome having someone I can truly look up to."

The heron leaned over, took him in its beak and swallowed the frog before he could utter another word.

"Already things are looking up under this King's reign," said the older frog—but then *he* was eaten too.

The heron was soon making a great feast of his subjects, and many frogs, wondering if service to the King should really include satisfying his appetite, hopped for their lives.

This was to no avail. They were all, in the eyes of their King, equally tasty and they were also equal in death.

The Miser

There was once a merchant who hated nothing more than spending money.

"That miser will be the death of me," his wife told anyone who would listen. "As night follows day, he will grumble about the cost of my funeral."

Those words were prophetic, for she indeed grew old before her time, worn out by the effort of nagging and pleading with her husband for the trappings of a life worthy of their class. When she died, the merchant complained bitterly.

"Expensive in life and just as expensive in death," he told his brother. "I thank god that she did not bear any children."

By means of the woman's persistence, however, the couple had gradually accumulated many fineries.

She had purchased jewellery and silk so that she could socialise with other merchants' wives without feeling like a poor village girl. She had bought glassware and bone china so that they might host dinners for visiting traders. She had filled their house with ornaments and art.

With the extreme care she had been forced to exercise in her spending, the woman had always sought expert advice. As a result, much of what she bought had increased enormously in value over the years of their marriage.

The merchant himself, however, attached little value to any of these possessions. He had spent a lifetime trading goods for gold, and he soon decided that this was exactly what he would do with all that he now owned.

He sold his wife's jewellery and the art that hung on the walls of his house. He sold furniture, china, even books. Finally he sold the house itself, buying instead a tiny cabin on the edge of town. With all his cash, he purchased an ingot of solid gold.

The merchant loved that gold more than he had ever loved anything—including his long-suffering wife.

"Now," he thought to himself, "how can I keep my gold safe?"

He disliked banks, since they only made money from other people's hard work and good fortune. If he lodged his gold at a bank, they would charge for its safekeeping and he would only be able to see his gold during business hours.

For this reason, the merchant decided to hide his gold in a secret location not far from his little cabin.

One night, under the cover of darkness, he dug a hole beside an old stone wall. He lined it with fleece, placed the ingot inside and covered it in such a way that passers-by would never detect what lay below the surface.

It happened, however, that a farm labourer in a nearby field observed a number of the man's visits to the spot. Intrigued, he waited for an opportunity to investigate.

Upon exposing the hole, the labourer could not believe

his eyes. The riches it contained were far beyond anything he had ever imagined—but they were not beyond his capacity to remove. He promptly did so and was never seen in the region again.

When the merchant discovered the theft, he started tearing at his hair. He wailed so loud, and for so long, that many presumed that his wife's death had belatedly struck at his emotions. His wife's family, still in mourning, sent the man's brother-in-law to console him. Grief shared, they thought, would aid in his recovery.

The brother-in-law fumed silently as the merchant told him of the only loss that had ever caused him pain—the gold he had loved and hidden in vain.

Finally, the brother-in-law could contain himself no longer.

"My family grieves for the woman who was your faithful wife," he began. "*Your* suffering, on the other hand, is attached to an object. It has neither lived nor died. I say to you—take a stone, place it in that hiding place of yours, and convince yourself it is gold."

"What value has a stone?" countered the merchant.

"Your gold has no more value than a stone, if you make not the slightest use of it."

With that, the brother-in-law rose from his chair. He left the merchant's cabin and never spoke to the miser again.

The Fox and the Goat

A fox is as proud as it is cunning—and pride, when extreme, can lead to a fall. Few foxes are so careless as to fall into a well, but such peculiar events are not unheard of.

One young fox, light on his feet and possessing fine balance, wanted more than anything to see himself in motion.

"What a glorious sight that must be," he told other foxes. "It is so terribly unfair that you can freely witness my grace—but that I, myself, cannot!"

Other foxes believed there was little point telling this fellow that he moved in a manner typical of their species, and that he could get the general idea by watching any one of them.

Consequently, the fox himself devised a plan. He would go to a nearby well and leap across it, watching his reflection in the water as he did so. It was this hare-brained scheme that led to the accident.

On the fox's fifth jump, he tried to reproduce the action of running while still in the air. Intent on catching a glimpse of this in the mirror below, he misjudged his landing and tumbled rather ungracefully into the well.

The fox was fortunate. The water was deep enough to cushion his landing—yet wasn't too deep for him to stand in. He felt foolish, and hoped no other fox had witnessed the incident. At that moment, his greatest fear was that he would become a laughing stock.

Then, far greater fears seized him. His mind raced as he considered his plight.

How will I get out of here? Even if another fox witnessed my fall, what could it do? Our kind is not known for its expertise with ropes and pulleys.

I cannot jump high enough to reach the top—not even if I had the advantage of a good run-up.

These walls are impossible for me to climb. Might I starve?

There and then, the fox realised that he needed to make full use of his intelligence. Whereas previously he had exercised little care and even less brainpower, these and these alone could now save him. And if he should survive, he decided, he would never forget his lesson.

A day passed and, try as he might, the fox was unable to conceive a plan that would save him. Cold and hungry though he was, however, he did not give up.

Finally, he heard the rasping voice of a goat from above.

"Good fellow," the goat said. "I'm dreadfully thirsty. How is the water?"

The fox thought quickly.

"Clean and refreshing! Come in, come in! Perhaps this water even has some magical property, for it has given me wisdom. I was once an old and mangy fox, would you believe? Now look at my coat—a little wet, but *magnificent*. I feel young again, young enough to..."

Before the fox could conclude his attractive advertisement of the well, the goat jumped in beside him. The parched goat drank as if the water might evaporate if he paused for even an instant.

The fox was pleased with this turn of events. He watched the goat with satisfaction.

"You see? You may never feel thirsty again."

The goat could only nod a little as he drank.

Eventually, however, he lifted his head and gave out a loud sigh of contentment. "Thank you, sir. I needed that!" Then the goat looked up. "Now, what is the best way to get out?"

"That is a matter I have considered most carefully," said the fox. He spoke with authority—for, indeed, a plan had been forming in his mind since the first appearance of the

goat. “First, you will help me by acting as a stepladder. Once I am out, I will pull you up to the top.”

To the goat, this sounded reasonable. He stood on his hind legs and rested his front hooves against the wall. The fox scrambled up the gullible goat’s shoulders and steadied himself before, with one mighty effort, leaping out of the well.

He turned to the goat. “Farewell, my friend, and thank you for your assistance.”

“You cannot leave!” the goat protested. “We had a plan. You must now help me!”

“Even if I should have the brute strength and the implements required to hoist you out, I would think twice,” the fox gloated. “After all, I found myself in the well by accident but you dived in like a fool. Had you examined the situation, you might have seen the need for an exit plan. You exposed yourself to dangers from which you had no means of escape.”

With that, the fox shook water from his coat and set off in the direction of a henhouse. The sun and freedom warmed him to the core.

Other books by Ken Spillman

ALL-TIME FAVOURITE

Fairy Tales 5-In-1: Vol 1

Ken Spillman

Illustrated by Beth Parrocha

Here's a collection of some of the best known tales for children delightfully retold by Ken Spillman. This brilliantly illustrated volume includes:

• Sleeping Beauty • Jack and the Beanstalk
• The Ugly Duckling • Cinderella
• The Three Little Pigs

ISBN: 9789351037002
Pages: 92
Format: PB; colour

ALL-TIME FAVOURITE

Fairy Tales 5-In-1: Vol 2

Ken Spillman

Illustrated by Beth Parrocha

In All-time Favourite Fairy Tales, children's author Ken Spillman retells five much-loved children's stories:

• Snow White and the Seven Dwarfs • Little Red Riding Hood
• Hansel and Gretel • Goldilocks and the Three Bears • Beauty and the Beast

Artist Beth Parrocha adds her own magic to the illustrations.

ISBN: 9789351037699
Pages: 96
Format: PB; colour

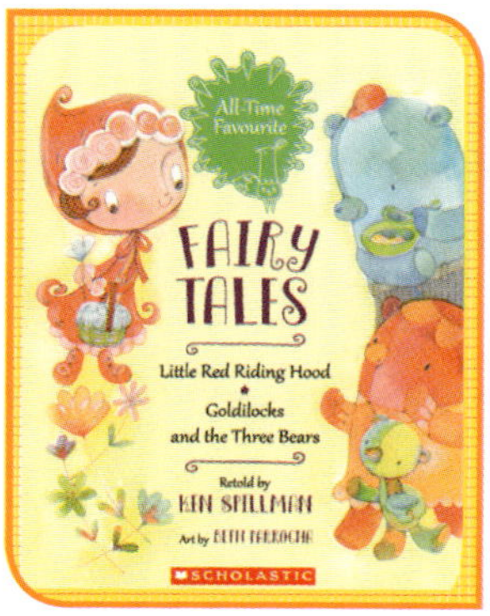

ALL-TIME FAVOURITE

Fairy Tales 2-In-1: Vol 1

Ken Spillman

Illustrated by Beth Parrocha

In All-time Favourite Fairytales, children's author Ken Spillman retells two much-loved children's stories:

• Little Red Riding Hood

• Goldilocks and the Three Bears

ISBN: 9789351038719
Pages: 32
Format: PB; colour

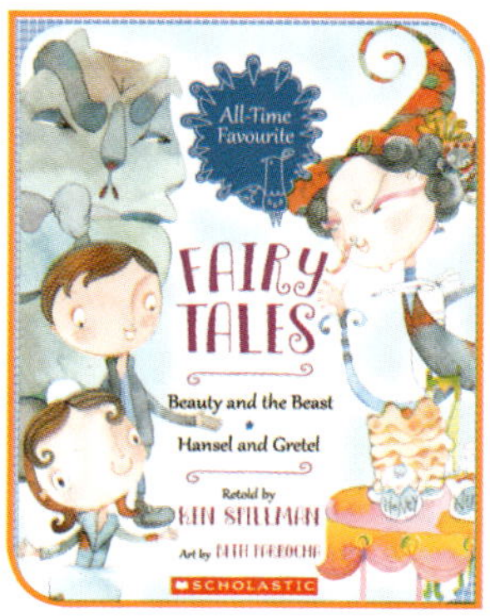

ALL-TIME FAVOURITE

Fairy Tales 2-In-1: Vol 2

Ken Spillman

Illustrated by Beth Parrocha

In All-time Favourite Fairytales, children's author Ken Spillman retells two much-loved children's stories:

• Beauty and the Beast

• Hansel and Gretel

ISBN: 9788184778021
Pages: 52
Format: PB; colour